Walt Disney's MICKEY AND FRIENDS
LET'S GO to the Dairy Farm

By Barbara Bazaldua
Illustrated by DiCicco Digital Arts

A GOLDEN BOOK • NEW YORK

Golden Books Publishing Company, Inc., New York, New York 10106

© 1998 Disney Enterprises, Inc. All rights reserved. Printed in the U.S.A. No part of this book may be reproduced or copied in any form without written permission from the copyright owner. A GOLDEN BOOK®, A LITTLE GOLDEN BOOK®, G DESIGN™, and the distinctive gold spine are trademarks of Golden Books Publishing Company, Inc. Library of Congress Catalog Card Number: 97-76886   ISBN: 0-307-98224-6   A MCMXCVIII   First Edition 1998

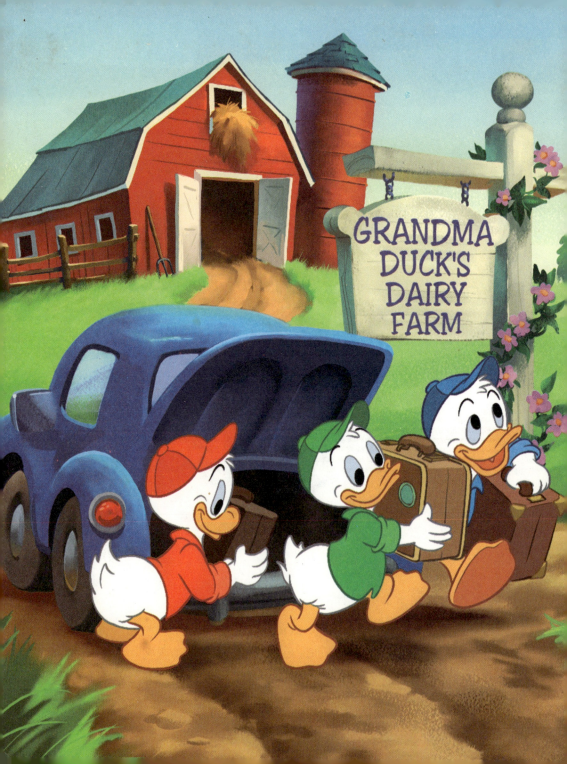

"Here we are at Grandma Duck's dairy farm," Donald said to his nephews Huey, Dewey, and Louie one summer morning. Mickey was with them, too. They had all promised to take care of Grandma's cows while she was on vacation.

"Grandma Duck left us lemonade—and plenty of instructions," said Mickey.

"Who needs instructions?" Donald replied. "I already know all about cows."

Mickey read Grandma's list. "It says here to milk the cows in the morning, put them out to pasture to eat grass, and then take them to the barn for their evening milking."

"I knew that," Donald said. Whistling a cheerful tune, he headed for the pasture. Mickey followed with Huey, Dewey, and Louie.

Mickey and the boys found the cows drinking from the farm pond. Mickey gave the largest one a gentle pat to get her started toward the barn. The other cows followed.

Donald saw one last cow standing behind a big, round bale of hay. "Here cow, here cow!" he called. But the cow wouldn't come.

"I said, 'Here, cow!'" Donald yelled, stomping toward the big animal.

Mickey, Huey, Dewey, and Louie hurried over to see what was happening. There, next to the big cow, stood a little calf.

"Why, this must be Rosie and her new calf!" Mickey exclaimed. "Grandma mentioned them specially in her instructions."

"Grandma says to take Rosie's calf to the barn and help it drink from a bottle," Mickey said.

Donald tried to lead the calf in the direction of the barn. But Rosie blocked his way.

"Come on . . . move, you silly cow!" Donald ordered, trying to push Rosie aside. Rosie refused to budge, so Donald pushed again.

That made Rosie mad. Bellowing angrily, she pushed him back. A second later she was chasing Donald around the pasture!

Meanwhile Mickey and the nephews had led the little calf to the barn and fed it from a bottle. Then they put the calf in a straw-filled stall.

"When Donald gets Rosie into the barn, we'll milk her. Then she can snuggle with her calf," Mickey told the boys.

   Just then Donald dashed into the barn with Rosie close behind him. He raced into a milking stall with Rosie right on his heels. Donald slipped away from the big cow, slammed the stall door shut, and leaned against it.

   "Guess I showed *her* who's boss!" he said, wiping his forehead.

"You sure did!" Mickey agreed. He handed Donald a bucket of soapy water. "Now you can wash her before she's milked."

"Aw, phooey! Who ever heard of washing a cow?" Donald muttered. But he lugged the bucket into Rosie's stall.

Donald set the bucket down right behind Rosie.
Swish, swish! went Rosie's tail as she flicked it back and forth. *Plop!* went the tail as she dipped it into the soapy water. And *whap!* went the tail as Rosie smacked suds right in Donald's face!

Sputtering and muttering, Donald finally managed to get Rosie washed. He watched Mickey and the boys hook the other cows up to milking machines.

"Now *that* looks easy," he said. But when he tried it with Rosie, she pushed him over and started to run.

"Whoa!" Donald shouted, grabbing her by the tail.

"Watch out, Unca Donald!" Huey shouted as Rosie dragged Donald through the barn. Donald's feet got tangled in the hoses that carried the milk to the storage tank.

Snap! One of the hoses came loose. Milk sprayed everywhere, soaking Donald from head to toe and splashing in his eyes.

With milk in his eyes, Donald couldn't see a thing. He stumbled over hoses, boots, and milk cans and bumped into doors. Finally he put his foot straight into a bucket, tripped, and fell into a feed bin.

"Oof!" Donald gasped as he climbed out covered with bits of mashed grain. "Yuck!" He pulled pieces of wheat stalks out of his sleeves.

While Donald dripped and fumed, Mickey helped Huey, Dewey, and Louie catch Rosie. They tied her up and began to clean the barn.

But Donald wasn't about to quit yet. He grabbed an old milking stool and bucket and marched toward Rosie.

"I'm going to milk this cow the old-fashioned way—by hand!" he declared.

When Rosie saw Donald approaching, a sly glint came into her big, brown eyes. As soon as he got close enough, she gave a powerful kick—*thunk!*—and sent him flying through the air.

Donald landed—*splash!*—head first in a full milk can!

Mickey pulled Donald out of the can. "You've helped enough for today," he said, trying not to smile. "We'll finish milking Rosie."

Rosie behaved like a perfect lady while Mickey milked her and then when Huey, Dewey, and Louie put her in the box stall with her calf.

After their chores were finished, the gang trooped back to the house and sat down for a rest on the front porch.

Just then, Grandma Duck drove up. "I missed my cows too much to go on vacation," she explained.

"Hmph! I hope I never see another cow again as long as I live!" Donald said grumpily.

"That's too bad," Grandma said. "Look what I brought you."

She handed each one a box. When they saw what was inside, everyone began to laugh—even Donald. For in each box was a huge piece of milk chocolate, shaped just like a cow!